Dash and his 7 brothers and sisters were having so much fun running around in the grass and chasing each other. They were still little pups and this was only the fourth time they had been outside.

Running and chasing each other was so much fun!!!

It was so cool everything they saw was new to them. Butterflies, clouds, birds and police cars and sirens. WHAT? Well at least Dash loved looking at the police cars going down the road with lights and sirens.

Dash loved watching the birds fly.

But seeing a police car was the best of all

"That's what I am going to be a Police Dog" Dash said." No, you're not Dash"." Yes, I am"." No, you're not and I will tell you why". "You don't look like other police dogs" "So What" Dash said. "You're the wrong kind they are German shepherds and Malinois you're a giant schnauzer and they are a different color". "You don't look like them". Dash walked away and was so hurt by what they had said.

Another police dog different than Dash.

Dash was so sad that his brothers and sisters said he could not be a police dog because he looked different than the other police dogs.

Dash walked over to his mom and said "Mom I want to be a police dog but my brothers and sisters said I can't because I don't look like the other police dogs, I am not the same color as them".

"Come closer Dash" his mom said. She put her paw around Dash and said "Dash you can be anything you want to be". "And it makes no difference how you look or what color you are we are all the same in Gods eyes"." Don't pay them any attention". "They love you very much and if you become police dog, they will be proud just like me and your dad will be".

The next day while Dash and his family played outside, he saw a bird splashing in a bird bath. It looked like fun. Dash went over to the bird and said "That looks like fun" "It is fun" the bird said. "My name is Dash and I am going to be a police dog". "Really" said the bird. "Then you should visit the police station its just down the road". "Really" Dash said. "Yep, it sure is I fly over it all the time".

Dash's new friend telling him where the police station is.

Dash looked around, his mom and dad had gone back into the house and his siblings were busy playing. He decided to take a chance. He found a place in the fence he could squeeze through. Two seconds later he was out of the yard. He knew he had to make the trip quick.

Dash squeezing through the fence.

Dash ran as fast as he could and as he ran around the curve, there it was, the police station. Wow it looked so neat!! He walked up to the front door and looked around. There were police cars and police trucks and whoops a policeman walking right toward him. "Hey little buddy you lost?" the police officer looked like a superhero. Dash though yep this is where I want to Be!!!!!

The inside of the police car was really cool. It had all kinds of lights and buttons and switches. He listened to the officers talk on the police radios.

Dash looked at the inside of the police car it was so cool !!!!!!!

Dash going home in the police car.

When Dash got home his mom was upset but not angry. "Dash you no better" she said. That night Dash had a dream about being a police dog and it was so neat.

Dash on his second trip to the police department.

A couple of days later Dash could not stand it he had to go back and visit the police station. He got through the fence and ran straight to the police departments front door. He was looking through the glass inside the police station when he heard "Hey little guy you back again?" It was his police buddy that he met he before Dash was jumping with excitement that he remembered Dash. The officer said "You must like this place let me give you a tour before I take you home".

It was so cool inside all the Officers were so nice. The officer them took Dash out back and said "Look little guy that is where we train the police dogs". It was so neat it was like a giant playground it had ramps and jumps and all kinds of things to climb on and through. The tour was the best ever.

Police dogs training on the obstacle course.

After the tour the officer drove Dash home again. This time the officer spent some time talking to the family that took care of Dash and his family. The officer told them in a few months he was going to start in the police k9 unit. The officer told the couple he did not have a dog yet and why not give Dash a shot at the position.

Officer asking Dash family to let for Dash to start Police Training.

The couple said, "But Dash is just a few months old" The officer explained to them that know training started when they were puppies. The couple laughed and said sure he is just going to run to the Police Department every time he is out anyway.

Dash had no idea that his dream of becoming a police dog was about to come true.

"Hey Dash come here" the officer yelled. Dash stopped why was he yelling my name? "Come here buddy" the officer said. Dash ran as fast as he could. When he got to the officer the officer bent down and said "How would you like to live with me and become a police dog? Oh my gosh really, really Dash thought? Sure, Sure as he ran beck to tell his brothers and sisters an told them he was going to live with his friend and become a police dog. "Really" they said? Yep. Dash hated to leave them but he was living his dream.

"Hey they are yelling for me YES" said Dash.

Dash hugging his family goodbye.

Dash went home with the officer and not only got to train to be a police dog but got to live with the officer and his family. He loved to play peek a boo with his mom. Sometimes for fun she would dress Dash up and say he made detective.

Dash palying dress up thinking he is a detective.

The months went by and one day a police car pulled into the driveway of Dash's old home. The officer got out and opened up the back door of his police car and out jumped a grown-up Dash. He was wearing a police badge on his collar. Dash had graduated first in his police k9 class. He was so proud and his family jumped with excitement. Dash ran to see them.

Dash running to see his family.

Dash's Graduation picture from the Police Dog Academy!!!!

Dash's brothers and sisters yelled "Dash you did it Dash you did it" Dash proudly told his siblings to just remember what their mom had said "You can be anything you want to be no matter how you look we are all the same in Gods eyes"

Please follow Dash in his series of children's books. Through Dash we hope to show children how to cope with being different, bullying, parents' divorce and other struggles they may face growing up. Dash is a real-life police dog in Louisville, Ky.

The Author Dennis Clark and Dash's partner has been a K9 Handler for over 30 years he recently authored the book shown below. Please check it out on Amazon.

LIFE SAVING
AWARD

Presented To

K-9 Dash

In Recognition of Your Actions
In The Saving of Another
Human Life, And For Handling An
Emergency With Uncompromised
Competence And Integrity.

West Buechel Police Department

K9 Dash

Dash's Certifications